NEVER BEEN KISSED

CONNOR WHITELEY

No part of this book may be reproduced in any form or by any electronic or mechanical means. Including information storage, and retrieval systems, without written permission from the author except for the use of brief quotations in a book review.

This book is NOT legal, professional, medical, financial or any type of official advice.

Any questions about the book, rights licensing, or to contact the author, please email connorwhiteley@connorwhiteley.net

Copyright © 2024 CONNOR WHITELEY

All rights reserved.

DEDICATION
Thank you to all my readers without you I couldn't do what I love.

CHAPTER 1
15th April 2023
Rochester, England

Sam Faircraft had always, always loved his family's ability to make any situation, event or news into a brilliant party. Sam was rather proud to admit that his entire family were rather well-known for their parties, their events and their laughter. It was why his parents were so popular and thankfully Sam was really popular at school because of it.

Because, what teenager didn't love a party?

Sam leant against the rough, warm bark of the huge apple tree in his equally large garden at his parent's house and just grinned at the great party around him. The garden was filled with impressive exotic trees that he had loved hiding behind as a child.

Monkey Puzzles, Figs and even Palm trees lined the centre of the garden as it gently sloped downhill. There was a vegetable patch to one side that Sam liked to tend to but it seemed that his peas and carrots had already been devoured by his little nephews and nieces as they sat in another corner of the garden stuffing their faces.

Sam seriously couldn't blame them. There was nothing like the wonderfully refreshing taste of garden peas picked just moments ago.

On the other side of the garden, Sam was glad to see all his uncles, aunts and other family members in their long sweeping summer dresses and black suits, were all looking at the flowers. Sam didn't know what most of the orange, blue and red flowers were called. He only knew they were expensive and beautiful to look at.

Everyone was laughing, talking and singing in the garden thanks to the massive karaoke machine his older brother had brought for the party. The entire excuse for the party had come from his recent Coming Out as gay but that thankfully hadn't changed anything.

It had just given his Mum and Dad an excuse to test out their brand-new barbeque.

Sam waved at his Mum as she came from their large masonry house at the top of the garden next to their fish pond and water fountain. He smiled as he remembered some of his aunts threatening to kindly throw their kids in the fishpond if they didn't behave.

Now that would be a sight to see considering how passive, loving and caring his aunts were.

"You trying to escape," Isla said as she came over to Sam and leant against the other side of the tree.

Sam was really glad his best friend in the entire world had wanted to come tonight. Granted she was always going to come because she was amazing and the bestest friend Sam could ask for. But she did look impressive in her flowery summer dress that showed off her long legs perfectly.

He was almost surprised his brothers hadn't hit on her yet.

"I could say the same to you," Sam said smiling.

"I just want to get away from Toby for a moment. Ever since he broke up with Aleshia he hasn't stopped texting me. I think he's looking for pity sex,"

Sam laughed, because that was probably true.

"Well, we'll be back at university next month for exams and then we can get away from Toby together," Sam said.

Sam smiled as one of his Dad's best friends in a navy blue suit gave him a funny look.

But now he was officially Out he couldn't deny how excited he was going back to university properly in September for his third and final year. He finally felt like he could join the LGBT+ society, go out to gay bars and just meet cute boys.

"You know," Isla said smiling, "you are Out now so you could finally do something about never being kissed,"

Sam rolled his eyes. "You love teasing me with that fact, don't you?"

"Well it is a highlight of my social life. That I've been kissed more than you considering the gay jokes around how many people gay people kiss,"

Sam couldn't exactly deny he had heard the same rumours but he was sure (or at least liked to believe) that they were mostly just rumours. But he would be lying if he said he didn't want to kiss people.

He was Out now. He was free to be okay, to live a gay life and just explore what being gay meant to him. Sam knew he could go up to London, go to a gay club and get laid twenty times over but he didn't want that.

Sam really, really wanted to be kissed by a man he cared about and someone who cared about him in return.

"How did you get your first kiss?" Sam asked, adjusting himself because a piece of bark was starting to dig into him.

"You were there, remember? You, me, kris and Thorn were hanging out in the canteen. I caught Drew Andrews looking at me, I gestured him over and he kissed me,"

"And that's how you allowed your boyfriend of four years. Yes, yes I know the story," Sam said really happy for his friend.

"Anyway beautiful we need to get you a kissing experience," Isla said knowing how happy he was for her. "We need to find you a nice guy to kiss, but someone that cares about you,"

Sam shrugged. He was so new to the gay world,

the gay scene and even at the university he had avoided a lot of the LGBT+ stuff because he was a little scared by it all. It wasn't like he could contact anyone to get information or even start chatting up.

"I know we've been at university for two years but was anyone gay at school?" Isla asked.

Sam nodded at his Mum as she came over with a tray full of small glasses of rum. Sam took one just to be nice, he had no intention of drinking the liquid fire.

"What about Mathew Harris?" Isla asked.

Sam grinned. Now that was a boy he could happily let kiss him until he sucked out all of his oxygen. Sam had always had a thing for Mathew. He was just so sexy, so damn beautiful and so clever like he was.

"He's straight," Sam said.

Isla leant forward like she was going to reveal nuclear launch codes or something.

"That might not be true. I kept in contact with some of our old school friends and there is a rumour round that Mathew is very interested in boys and girls. You might want to contact him,"

Sam shook his head. He didn't want to contact an extremely hot schoolfriend that he hadn't spoken to for two years, and even before that their conversations had been limited.

"Do you want to kiss someone hot or not?"

Damn it. Sam really didn't like it when Isla knew him too well so he nodded, took out his phone and found Mathew on Social media.

And he started typing out a message.

After this Sam just knew he was so going to be downing the liquid fire. Of that there was no doubt.

CHAPTER 2
17ᵗʰ April 2023
London, England

Mathew Harris had always enjoyed living, working and doing adult things in London. He just loved the culture, the clubs and he really, really liked his job at Frank's Marketing Agency. It was a great company, very friendly and Mathew had to admit he did get a lot of great marketing projects thrown at him.

Mathew sat at his very modern, expensive and charming glass desk with his computer open on a whole bunch of emails from morning meetings and other rubbish that had come up over the weekend.

Mathew closed the emails' tab and just admired his large modern office that a lot of junior professionals would have killed to have. It was easily large enough to have a party inside, and normally he had departmental meetings in here and everyone enjoyed the teal fabric sofas and the stunning views of

London.

He really liked the views himself, not that he got a lot of time to admire them. He could see the swirling, churning River Thames, all the commuter traffic below him and he could see the wonderful landmarks. Like the London Eye, the Houses of Parliament and Tower Bridge.

It was great to look out of the huge floor-to-ceiling windows on a summer's day.

The large mug of lukewarm coffee from the coffee woman downstairs made the entire office smell of rich bitter rich with delightful hints of caramel, toffee and nutmeg. It was the perfect way to approach a Monday morning when one of his projects was falling well and truly apart.

He took a mouthful of the coffee and enjoyed the sheer explosion of flavour in his mouth, he really couldn't get enough of that toffee.

By the time he had left the office Friday night he had scheduled models, a photoshoot and meetings with the huge Fashion Company they were meant to be doing marketing for. But over the weekend the models had cancelled because someone else who was paying them more had hired them instead.

So the models went elsewhere.

Mathew wouldn't have minded that at all, because these things happen. But when the photographer jumped ship too because he had been sacked and the photo company had failed to offer a replacement, Mathew felt like his entire career was collapsing around him.

Someone pounded on the frosted glass door of his office and Mathew just rolled his eyes.

There was only one person it could be. His boss Miranda.

Mathew couldn't even say *come in* before Miranda in her black business suit that made her look like an assassin was already half way across the office towards him.

She sat down and Mathew felt like he was about to be punished like he had been at school.

"Good morning Mathew," Miranda said in her normal cold business tone that Mathew wasn't a fan of. "Thank you for your morning briefing and that is the only reason why I am not shouting at you. You are honest, you are a good worker and you are… effective at your job,"

Mathew imagined that was exactly what assassins said to each other.

"You didn't work your way to this position as Department Senior within two years to destroy your career now, did you?"

"What?" Mathew asked not understanding what was happening.

"The Diamond Fashion Company is a multi-billion pound company with quarterly campaigns. Each paying us five million each time. I am not allowing this company to slip through our fingers. If there is not a campaign delivered to the customer's satisfaction by the deadline of this Friday then believe me. Your head is rolling,"

Mathew laughed nervously. He couldn't find any more models, any more photographers and still get it all together before Friday.

Miranda stood up. "You are one of the most resourceful people I know Mr Harris. I have stressed to the board that everything is well in hand but I do require updates every four hours otherwise I will sack you as a gesture of goodwill,"

"I didn't know you were in trouble with your own Board," Mathew said.

Miranda frowned. "Focus on yourself or you might be joining me on benefits,"

Mathew nodded his goodbyes to Miranda and he held his stomach as it twisted into a painful knot.

This seriously couldn't be happening. He had dedicated the last two years of his life to this company, he had loved the work and he had loved doing his online business degree on the side at night.

He couldn't lose this job.

Mathew took a deep breath of the coffee-scented air and checked his social media for the first time in days to give himself a break. Then hopefully this would refresh him to tackle this dire problem.

Mathew noticed he had a new message and he was surprised it was from Sam Faircraft. He just grinned because Sam had always been a hot guy back at school even when he was technically overweight by a lot.

But Mathew clicked on his social media profile

by accident and he was really, really pleased at how hot, sexy and cute Sam looked now. It looked like he had lost a ton of weight and he looked even more amazing.

He even looked model-like.

Mathew read the message and he had never expected Sam to be gay and he was asking if they would go out for dinner sometime.

Mathew wasn't exactly opposed to a date at all because Sam was cute, it had been ages since he had got on a real date instead of a hookup and if he was being really honest with himself then he had always *liked* Sam a lot more than he should have.

And he seriously needed someone with model-like features.

Mathew leant back in his chair. He had done photoshoots with a single model before and Sam wasn't stupid. He had always been a very fast learner so it wouldn't be hard to teach him exactly what he needed to be.

Mathew grinned as he remembered just how helpful Sam liked to be too. Mathew supposed if he made it sound like Sam was doing him a massive favour then Sam might volunteer for the photoshoot himself.

And save Mathew's career in the first place.

Mathew sent a reply and his stomach filled with butterflies at the very idea of seeing his very hot and model-like friend from school.

Little did Mathew realise just how badly this was

going to bite him in the ass later on.

CHAPTER 3
17th April 2023
London, England

Sam really supposed he knew he didn't have much of a life outside of university, his student ambassador job and helping his older brother coach a football team, when he realised he could easily drop everything to travel up to London to have dinner with a boy he seriously liked.

He had driven up to London easily enough and Sam was currently standing outside a very posh, slightly expensive restaurant that he had never would have considered going to himself, but Mathew had said he was paying and Sam had no problem with that.

Sam leant against the slightly warm cream-coloured marble that pulsed a little bit of warmth through his light green jacket, blue jeans and Chelsea boots. He hadn't wanted to go overboard for the catch-up but he also didn't want Mathew to think he hadn't achieved much since school.

Sam watched as straight couples went in and out of the golden metal doors of the restaurant in long sweeping dresses, suits and trousers. The couples looked so happy, cheerful and like this was the start of an amazing night tonight.

Sam really hoped that was going to happen to him as well.

The street itself was wide and rather quiet for a London street. Sam had been to London tons of times before and he was almost surprised at the lack of black cabs, buses and cars on the road.

The setting evening sun shone bright and lit up everything whilst giving it a great orange-tint at the same time. Sam really liked how the air smelt refreshing of pine, freshly roasted, juicy pork and crispy fish ready to be enjoyed.

Sam was so looking forward to having dinner with such a beautiful man. He had really missed Mathew over the past two years.

Mathew had always been the super clever one, the sporty one and he was just the hot sensationally perfect guy that Sam had always wanted to be and date and kiss.

It was actually Mathew that had made Sam realise he was gay. When Sam had been 13, he had been standing outside the school library with the rest of his class for "reading time" and then he had seen Mathew for the first time ever.

Sam still couldn't stop how fit, hot and stunning

Mathew had looked with his blond hair and sporty body. Mathew had been perfect then and he hadn't changed at all during their time at school together.

Sam's phone buzzed and he was glad Isla had called him.

"So is what he like?" Isla asked.

Sam rolled his eyes. "He hasn't turned up yet. It's 6 pm now. He said he would turn up any time now and, why are you so interested?"

"Because I might be on a date with Toby," Isla said clearly embarrassed.

Sam laughed. He shouldn't have doubted that Toby would eventually wear his best friend down, but he knew deep down that Isla liked his brother too. There was a minor age gap of three years but he had seen the way Toby looked at Isla and vice versa, they did like each other.

The only problem was that until now neither one wanted to admit it.

"Have a great time. I know my brother is a bit of a handful but he is a lovely guy. He cares about you but tell him if he's being a dick,"

"Are you trying to make me worried?"

Sam laughed. "No just doing little brother stuff,"

"Have fun and call me when you get home," Isla said in-between laughing.

"You to," Sam said hanging up and then he looked up and his entire world changed.

Sam just stared as walking towards him was the most beautiful, sexy, divine man he had ever seen. His heart pounded in his chest. His dick flared to life. Sam's mind went blank.

All he could do was focus on the hot, confident man walking towards him.

Sam had to admit Mathew had always looked sensational in a suit. But tonight, Mathew looked even more like a God than he had back at school. Mathew had grown taller but his black business suit still looked as fitted and highlighted his incredible body as normal.

Sam could still see the outline of Mathew's wonderfully fit body through his blazer being unbuttoned. He didn't have a six-pack or muscles but Sam really didn't care. Mathew was just so lean, fit and Sam loved how sporty his legs looked.

Sam noticed as Mathew turned slightly so he didn't bump into a woman and her friend that his ass was just as large, solid and divine as all those years ago. And Mathew's square face with his seriously model-like jawline was perfect, as was his blond hair.

Sam so badly wanted to, needed, longed to kiss him like he had wanted to do so many times at school.

And this just might be his chance to finally let all his dreams come true.

CHAPTER 4
17th April 2023
London, England

Mathew had never felt so nervous, excited and happy in all his life as he went towards the restaurant where he was meeting beautiful Sam. As much as Mathew didn't want to admit it he had spent most of the afternoon admiring Sam's social media pictures. He was really cute now, even more so than he had been at school.

Mathew kept going down a busy London street. There were tons of little black cabs, buses and cars driving up with silly tourists running between them. The white block houses on either side of the road were clean, sterile and clinical like they always were. Mathew much preferred his apartment in one of the new skyscrapers in London because at least that had some character.

The evening crowd in London was always a little slow and relaxed and it was such a relief compared to the free-for-all that the London commute was. He had easily been knocked to the ground three different times on the commuter rush on Monday mornings.

But everyone in this crowd was slowly walking up and down wherever they needed to go. A lot of hot, sexy men were wearing tight-fitting business suits in shades of black, blue and grey. Whereas a lot of the slightly less prettier women were wearing dresses, blouses and trousers.

Mathew still couldn't believe that Miranda had jumped at the chance to have Sam stand in as the model and now that she was expecting him to deliver, Mathew supposed he couldn't fail.

He didn't want to admit that he was technically using Sam. Sam was just such a great guy, he was kind, wonderful and helpful with his sexy body that Mathew really wanted to kiss and explore.

But he still wanted to save his job. He needed the money to pay for the stupid rent that all Londoners had to pay for his tiny apartment, he needed the money to pay for his online degree and he needed money to live on.

He shook his head because he couldn't fail and as much as he didn't want to, if he had to technically use Sam to save his entire world and stop it crashing down. Then it was sadly something he was prepared to do because he didn't have another choice.

And Mathew had got in touch with his old school friend Isla and she had told him a whole bunch of things about Sam. He wanted someone to kiss him, like him and maybe even date.

Mathew had dated a lot of guys before, he had certainly kissed more than a hundred men and he was more than willing to kiss someone as beautiful as Sam.

"Watch it," a woman said as Mathew bumped into her.

Mathew nodded. He hadn't meant to get lost in his own thoughts so badly. At work and even in his personal life he was so focused, always focusing on the details and making sure that everything was perfect. He hadn't realised his attraction and lust for Sam might affect him this badly even before they had had their first date or whatever he wanted to call it.

He had no idea what Sam would think this was but he wasn't that surprised Sam had had a thing for him. Mathew had always caught Sam looking, smiling and flirting with him ever so slightly. Mathew hadn't minded at all because Sam had helped him realise he was into guys too.

All because Mathew had always liked Sam a lot more than he ever wanted to admit.

Mathew turned a street corner onto a wide London road that was certainly quieter and even the massive stream of people going and coming from different places seemed to thin out a lot. Allowing him to breathe for the first time in ages.

He kept going down the street until he saw Sam standing by the large golden metal doors of the restaurant.

And Mathew just knew he was going to get fucked. Maybe not by Sam but certainly by his job because Sam was way, way, way better in person than his social media pictures had ever revealed.

Mathew stumbled a little as he slowly went towards beautiful Sam.

Mathew couldn't believe how much better Sam's fashion sense had gotten in the past two years. His green jacket really bought out the colour of his stunning eyes, the jacket hugged Sam's seriously thin, slim, fit body that Mathew really wanted to touch. He would love to know how hard Sam's body was against his touch.

And Sam's face was smooth, thinned out and he just looked cute and innocent standing against the marble of the restaurant.

Mathew felt so nervous, embarrassed and shameful about his motives for tonight. But he was still more than glad what he was doing, because he was finally getting to have dinner with a man he had always had a crush on and he had really wanted to know was gay.

Mathew only hoped Sam had always been into him as Mathew had been into him.

CHAPTER 5
17th April 2023
London, England

Sam just grinned like a little schoolboy as Mathew came over and stopped right in front of him. He couldn't believe how horny he felt in the presence of such a hot, beautiful man that he had fantasized over since he was 13 years old.

He flat out loved Mathew's rich, earthy aftershave that made him smell so heavenly and manly. Sam really wanted to hug Mathew, kiss him and make Mathew push him up against the marble to kick off their magical evening together.

Then Sam forced himself to focus on how this wasn't a real date and they had only just reconnected. As much as he wanted something a lot more to happen, he had to remain in check and not let his horniness take over, no matter how impossible that was going to be.

"You look beautiful," Mathew said biting his

lower lip.

Sam felt his heart skip a few beats. He had never heard a guy say that about him before, it was great to hear.

"Thanks," Sam said feeling his smile might break his face soon. "You look amazing as always. Should we go in?"

Mathew nodded and Sam let him go first just so Sam could stare at his wonderful ass as they went towards their table. Sam was really glad his prediction earlier was right. Mathew's ass was just as good now as when they had been at school together.

A very young waitress led them through the very posh, modern restaurant. Sam liked it how all the little black glass tables were arranged in neat little rows whilst larger groups got to enjoy large blue, green or brown booths depending on their table.

The waitress took them up some black stairs up towards the back of the restaurant where a small table was already waiting for them with a romantic candle burning in the middle and two chairs already pulled out for them.

The sweet live classical music of the restaurant really made it feel posh, expensive and classy. Something Sam had never got to experience before, it was nice for a change but he was fairly sure he could never have enjoyed this every night of the week. It just wasn't normal.

"Can I push you in?" Mathew asked.

Sam so badly wanted to reply with what exactly

Mathew could push into him but he behaved himself, sat down and felt like a million dollars as Mathew was a gentleman and pushed his seat in.

Sam got another wonderful hit of that expensive aftershave and he knew he was going to have the best night of his life. He was actually on his first-ever gay date.

It was going to be brilliant.

"So what have you been up to since school?" Sam asked a little disappointed when Mathew sat down because he couldn't look at his ass anymore.

"I started my business degree with an online university and got a job up here for a marketing agency," Mathew said.

"Brilliant. I'm sure Mrs Eden would be happy one of her prized students went on to business," Sam said.

"I know you used to look at me in business studies a lot,"

Sam noticed how light-hearted and happy Mathew sounded so he decided the truth was better than lying.

"The advantages of you sitting opposite me on your computer," Sam said really happy he finally got to admit how much he liked Mathew.

Sam smiled at the waitress as she passed them the drinks menu and Sam ordered a Diet Coke and Mathew ordered himself an apple Tango. Sam had no idea how Mathew could even remotely like that weird taste.

"Do you know whatever happened to Mrs Eden? I tried to use her as a reference a while back but the school couldn't contact her,"

Sam nodded. "She moved up North so she could be closer to her parents and family. There was some sort of family emergency and Mrs Eden being her, always loves to help out people in need,"

"True to that," Mathew said. "What about you? Did you ever go to University College London like you wanted to?"

Sam laughed. "I couldn't imagine anything worse. Not because of the university, that's great but the cost of living in London is stupid. Some of my other friends went and wow, she had to pay £20,000 for a year's lease for a shared flat complex,"

Mathew shook his head and Sam felt so warm and happy that they were finally talking. He had dreamed a lot during school about talking, flirting and maybe even kissing Mathew's soft, sporty lips but that had sadly never happened but maybe it could now.

Sam really, really wanted it too.

"So I went Kent University instead. I like the course, made a lot of friends and hopefully I can make a lot more now that I'm Out," Sam said biting his lower lip because he was slightly unsure about how to approach the subject.

"I didn't know you were into men," Mathew said knowing he wasn't sure about approaching the subject. "Then again I guess you didn't know I was bisexual either. School was a weird time and I knew I could have come out a lot sooner but I hadn't realised how much I liked men until after we left Sixth Form,"

Sam nodded his thanks as the waitress bought them drinks.

"Why?" Sam asked after taking a sip of his Diet Coke.

Mathew grinned. "Because you weren't there anymore. I know we didn't exactly share many classes except Form time, Business Studies and that was it. But I did like you a lot more than I realised,"

Sam loved it as his stomach filled with butterflies and he couldn't help but grin. So he raised his glass of Diet Coke.

"To us and making up for the past," Sam said as they cheered each other.

"And hopefully a good future,"

Sam grinned and forced himself to take another sip so he didn't look like a smiling idiot because he really was having the best time and it was so great to see Mathew again and just talk gay stuff with him.

Something he had wanted to do for so, so long.

CHAPTER 6
17th April 2023
London, England

After an incredibly flavourful well-done steak with beautifully saluted vegetables with just the right hint of garlic mixed into the rich, creamy butter, Mathew had to admit he was having the best night of his life.

Him and Sam had spoken about tons of things ranging from their school days to their interest in men to everything in-between. In fact Mathew was rather surprised they had spoken more about life and school than any gay topics. He knew back when he had freshly Come Out as Bisexual he went through a period of about a month where he could only talk about sex stuff. He was amazed that his parents and brothers and sister hadn't moaned at him.

But Mathew was so glad tonight had been so nice, refreshing and it was great to just get back to his roots. Mathew hadn't realised how used to the business, chaos, party-like culture of London where he was always going out, in a rush or at some party in the evenings.

It was great to go out with an old hot schoolfriend, catch up and not have to almost perform to anyone.

Mathew hadn't realised until now that that was what he had always done in London. He had to perform to his bosses that he was an extremely well-educated and capable Junior Senior, he had to perform to his friends that he was a party boy that couldn't get enough of random guys and girls coming and going from his bedroom and he had to perform to everyone else. That he was okay when he actually wasn't sure.

If he hadn't been here tonight with beautiful Sam then Mathew supposed he would have been at the local gay sex club using the constant sex to hide his stress and concern about work. It wasn't healthy and Mathew was tempted to wonder about all the other unhealthy habits he had but he just took one long at sexy Sam and decided he owned it to himself to live in the moment.

The moment where all his dreams, interests and minor fantasies about him and Sam might actually happen.

"Tell me about work then," Sam said leaning forward after finishing a mouthful of his pork and ale pie, "what actually does a marketing agency do?"

Mathew smiled. More to force himself not to

show his own extreme guilt at the moment, this had been the moment he had been wanting to avoid like the plague. Yet it was also the perfect segway into asking Sam for help.

And basically using him just because Mathew wanted to save his job and life as he knew it.

"I'm a Junior Senior Manager at the company," Mathew said really getting passionate about his job. "So a company will come to us and talk to the Board, sometimes me directly. They will list out their aims, objectives and what they want us to do and then I need to make it happen,"

Sam didn't look like he understood. Mathew couldn't believe how damn adorable he looked.

"My current company is a bit of a disaster because I have a billion-pound company coming in and they want a full Summer Ad campaign done,"

Sam nodded.

"They need a campaign that shows the world how great their summer range looks. They need photos, videos and more of models wearing their clothing. All because the company wants to increase their sales by 100% during the summer period,"

"But they won't know until Autumn if their marketing worked," Sam said.

Mathew nodded. "Exactly so I came up with the background, the styling and the models for the campaign. Then I booked the photographer and everything else needed but the models have gone and so has the photographer,"

Mathew felt his stomach twist into a painful knot but as he looked into Sam's deep dark green eyes. And he saw Sam's grin around them, Mathew just felt all his stress melt away because he was with Sam.

He had no idea what was causing this reaction but he felt so relaxed, so calm and like he could take on the world when Sam was with him.

Mathew reached across the table and took Sam's hand in his. Even he was surprised by how wonderfully warm, soft and loving Sam's hands felt. Mathew wanted so badly to kiss Sam's hand, invite him back to his apartment and fuck him til morning.

But he couldn't.

Mathew flat out couldn't do that with Sam, because Sam was actually special. He wasn't some guy or girl he could pick up at a club, do at home and then never see them again. Not only because he doubted Sam could handle that sort of emotionless relationship with him never even having kissed a guy before. But because Mathew knew that if he wanted to have a good relationship based on respect, trust and longing with anyone then it was going to be with Sam.

The guy he cared about a lot more than he had ever cared about anyone else. Sam was special and that meant something to him.

"So what are you going to do?" Sam asked.

Mathew forced himself not to show his frustration at Miranda and what the Board was wanting him to do, so he just answered the question with a half-truth.

"I'm currently looking for other options. If you know any models or good looking people then please tell me,"

"I'm looking at one right here,"

Mathew grinned and felt his cheeks warm up but maybe that wasn't such a bad idea after all. If he did become the model for the campaign then it meant he wouldn't have to "use" Sam for his looks and he could still keep his job.

"For that lightning bolt let me buy you dessert," Mathew said feeling the happiest he had been for ages.

CHAPTER 7
18ᵗʰ April 2023
Rochester, England

Sam had flat out enjoyed last night's date with Mathew. He hadn't laughed, talked about everything and nothing and just enjoyed life that much for so, so long. Sure he loved his life and his family and he had always had a great time with Isla but last night was just something else.

Sam sat under the massive apple tree in his parents' garden as the evening sun started to set with Isla. She wore a rather revealing summer dress with red, purple and blue flowers so Sam was guessing that her date with Toby had gone well last night

The warm ground under him kept him warm and Sam really liked sitting there next to the apple tree. It was in a suntrap and he had always sat here in the evening on the ground ever since he was a kid. Sometimes he used to play with his toys here, other times he would think about life and some more times he just liked spending time with his friends here.

A warm evening breeze brushed his cheeks and made the branches above him bang together and Sam waved at Toby as he came towards them.

Sam had to admit that even Toby was looking a little transformed by his date last night. He was actually wearing clothes for starters and his jeans, white t-shirt and brand-new trainers (instead of 10-year-old ones) looked really good on him.

"So how well did this date go last night?" Sam asked not at all sure if they were boyfriend or girlfriend or whatever at this point.

Isla kissed Toby lightly on the cheek and then Toby sat down next to her and they hugged. Sam shook his head, they did make a cute couple that was for sure.

"It went really well," Isla said. "I didn't Toby would be such a sweetheart and I think it was just nice spending time with a normal guy,"

Sam laughed. "The very last thing I would ever call my brother is normal for starters. And you have dated good people before, I think I was even one of them,"

"True," Isla said smiling. "But we all knew you were gay so we all knew our relationship was of convenience,"

Sam nodded. That really was the truth but he was still more than glad they had managed to stay friends, he actually couldn't imagine life without Isla.

Sam rolled his eyes as he noticed his Mum was

coming down the garden carrying a massive white tray of lemonade for them to enjoy. It wasn't exactly summer yet so the drink might have been uncalled for, but he knew what his Mum really wanted.

She wanted information, to be nosy and just spend time with her children. And maybe even future daughter-in-law.

He shook at the very idea at Toby and Isla getting married but he loved Isla so he couldn't moan too much.

"How about your date?" Toby asked.

Sam grinned. He had been dying to tell someone all day but his parents and even Isla had this thing called work.

"Amazing. It was so great seeing Mathew again and he is bisexual too," Sam said not knowing if that mattered. It actually didn't but he wanted to give his family all the details. "And we're going back out together tomorrow,"

Sam could see that Toby wasn't too sure about the second date. Isla looked happy as always so he couldn't understand what Toby knew that he didn't, Toby had always hung round with that crowd back in secondary school but still.

"Are you sure you want to go out with *him* of all people?" Toby asked. "I was good friends with him at school and he is a player. He might be clever, I suppose beautiful and a great teammate in football. But a lot of people abandoned him from school,"

Sam nodded at his Mum and grabbed a tall thin

glass of homemade lemonade as she sat down next to them.

"Why would they abandon him?" Sam asked.

"Because I heard," his Mum said, "that he was too focused on his career and he forgot about his friends. And when he did remember that he had friends, he wanted to use them to further his career,"

Sam shook his head. He couldn't believe that. That sounded like an evil thing to do and that wasn't right at all. No one should ever use their friends just to further their career, Sam couldn't imagine ever doing that to Isla and his other friends.

He was friends with them because they were great people, not because they would be useful to his career. If he had wanted that he seriously needed to get some "better" friends.

"But how long ago was that?" Sam asked.

"Yeah," Isla said, "I suppose he could have changed. Just look at Toby here two days ago I was running away from him and now we're dating,"

Sam wasn't sure if she was mocking him or not. He hoped she wasn't, but if she was he did sort of get her point people didn't really change that much over two years.

"I'll be okay and if he does want anything from me I will simply say no," Sam said knowing that he was lying through his teeth.

He had never been with a man before, he had never been kissed and he had never been touched by a man before either. And as much as Sam flat out didn't want to admit it if the opportunity came up he really didn't know what lines he wouldn't cross to get a kiss.

Something he had never ever gotten before and he seriously wanted a kiss. Especially by someone as hot and perfect and sexy as Mathew.

CHAPTER 8
18th April 2023
London, England

As Mathew stood in his office overlooking the tall beauty of London's skyline in the evening, he couldn't believe he was so damn nervous about his meeting with Miranda that was about to start, or it was as soon as she decided to grace him with her presence.

Mathew focused on a large row of three red London buses as they worked their way through the busy London commuter traffic as did the black cabs and the rest of the various vehicles that fought their way through London. Those drivers were a lot braver than he was. He just preferred the Tube.

The sweet aroma of toffee, coffee and caramel filled the office from his massive mug of coffee he had grabbed for himself earlier that made the great taste of coffee cake form on his tongue. He didn't want this meeting, he didn't want any of this situation but he had to make sure he didn't need to use Sam at all.

Mathew really liked Sam. He was cute, funny and such an amazing guy that all that Mathew wanted to do was catch up and make up for lost time together. They simply couldn't have dated during secondary school but there was a real chance for them to be a couple, boyfriends and something loving right now.

"Evening," Miranda said as she gave in.

Mathew turned around and was shocked to see Miranda had decided to bring in the entire board with her that all looked identical to each other minus their clothing options. Mathew had never seen most of the twenty men and ten women before in their tight black suits, black dresses and blouses and trousers. They all looked a million dollars and he was a poor person compared to them.

He didn't have enough seats so he simply stood there and he made sure to smile as he spoke. But his confident so wasn't there.

"As you are all aware we are in a crisis situation because the Fashion Company situation and we have no models and no photographer," Mathew said.

"Correction," a young man said, "you are in a crisis situation because Miranda warned you about this modelling agency and you decided to ignore the advice of a superior,"

"She did no such thing," Mathew said by accident and realised even though Miranda had lied to the board, it was a stupid thing to do to actually challenge her about it.

The oldest man in the room looked at Miranda. "I told you all that she is a liar and a trickster and she will be the death of this company,"

Miranda frowned at Mathew. "What have you got for us then? You must have been working on a solution because your updates were hopeful,"

"I think we can run a single model campaign effectively for the Fashion Company using myself as the model instead of my first idea," Mathew said really wanting to protect beautiful Sam.

"Impossible," Miranda said as she banged on about the specifications of the campaign.

Mathew went over to his desk and hated how his mug was empty and he hated it even more when the damn Board members started nodding along with her.

"Actually," Mathew said wanting to save himself, "you signed off on the idea of Sam being the model yourself. That is a single model campaign and you were fine about it then. Why does Sam have to be the model?"

Miranda laughed. "Because you are ugly and you are nothing and your contract does not allow it,"

The oldest man in the room came over to Miranda and Mathew recognised him now as the Chairman of the Marketing Agency. A recent replacement of Miranda now the Board had lost confidence in her.

"Whilst I do completely agree with Miranda's assessment of Sam compared to you. I would like to remind Miranda that calling employees ugly is wrong and I will not tolerate it and due to a motion passed by the board in your absence early you are sacked effective immediately Miranda,"

Miranda gasped. Her hands formed fists and then she simply relaxed.

"I will fight this," Miranda said being escorted out the office by three security men.

The oldest man looked at Mathew. "That means a position is available for you on the Board of Directors if you pull off this campaign. If you fail then the old deal still stands we need the Fashion Company's business we cannot fail. If you fail, you are out and I will blacklist you from this industry,"

Mathew nodded and just collapsed into one of the large sofas around his office as the Board members left. He couldn't believe this was happening, he couldn't believe that Miranda had finally been sacked for lying to the Board and that he could actually become a Board member.

That would be flat out amazing.

Mathew had heard about the benefits of the Board for the past two years. So many doors opened up around London and the entire marketing world, it gave him power and he would finally never have to worry about money ever again.

He could pay for his degree outright and just enjoy life to the fullest.

Then Mathew realised that if he ever wanted to achieve his wildest dreams he really, really needed to convince Sam to become a model for him and that meant telling him a lie or two or three.

Mathew hated this part of the job because he really liked Sam. And all Mathew wanted to do was love, kiss and have an amazing relationship with Sam.

He could have all of that after the promotion but he had three days to get the campaign together.

Time was running out to achieve everything he ever wanted.

Little did Mathew realise that no one ever gets everything they want in life and he would be no exception in the end.

CHAPTER 9
19th April 2023
Strood, England

For their next date, Sam had really, really wanted to go back to their teenage roots a little so he had wanted to go bowling at a place that was local, fun and all the popular kids used to come to during secondary school.

Sam sat in the small reception area of the immense Bowling's Heaven bowling alley on a hard red plastic seat that really did nothing to support Sam's body. He was glad he was in perfect health and had a tiny body otherwise he would have hated to imagine how much pain he would be in.

The reception itself was nice enough. There was a large bowling-themed wooden desk to his left where three young women sat around talking and there were large glass doors in front of him allowing him to watch all the young families, girlfriends and boyfriends bowl together.

There was a young family closest to the door made of a mum, dad and three teenage daughters. Sam smiled as one was on her phone and clearly having a text argument with someone but the other two were laughing and shouting well done to each other.

Sam really liked that everyone was having a great time spending an evening together with their loved ones at bowling.

Sam had never really been much of a bowler as a teenager. He had had the friends to do it but they all preferred to do other things on weekends and had just never got round to bowling.

He was so glad that was finally changing.

Mathew came through the door next to him, they hugged and Sam flat out loved the keep tenderness, passion and unsolved sexual tension in the hug. He so badly wanted the hug to turn into a kiss but Mathew felt really tense and stressed and then he went to check in. And grab them both some bowling shoes.

Sam watched the beautiful man he had longed for for so long. He seriously looked amazing in his white shirt, black trousers and black shoes so he had probably just come down from London without changing and Sam really hoped Mathew would be too tired to go back to London, so he would have to stay the night.

The horror. Not.

Sam grinned at Mathew as he passed him some bowling shoes that Sam laughed at. He had never understood why bowling shoes needed to look so clownish and horrible but he supposed that was all part of the fun.

"How was work?" Sam asked putting on his shoes.

Mathew laughed. "Don't even go there. It's a nightmare at the moment because I might be getting a job promotion but I need to pull off a marketing campaign,"

"The one without the models and photographers," Sam said wanting Mathew to know he listened to him.

"Good memory," Mathew said standing up and Sam just laughed at him in his bowling shoes.

The bowling shoes so didn't work with his stunningly hot business outfit. Sam so badly wanted to kiss him, Mathew looked amazing.

Sam followed Mathew through the glass doors and to their bowling lane on the far side of the alley.

Sam typed in their names into the machine and he couldn't believe but wonder if Mathew was going to try and use him to advance his career like Toby had said about. Sam doubted it because someone with Mathew's looks, charm and sheer divine aura could get anyone.

It made no sense whatsoever for Mathew to want to use Sam. He shook the stupid idea away because Toby was probably just being too overprotective like a brother should be.

Sam stood to one side as Mathew grabbed a

bowling ball.

"How's your life going?" Mathew asked.

"Good thanks. It's the Easter break so I have a month off uni then it's exams and I'm off til September for my final year. I'm excited. How's your online degree going?"

Sam could see Mathew shift nervously and as he released the bowling ball and it went into the gutter. Sam knew he clearly didn't like talking about it.

"Not going well?" Sam asked.

"No it isn't that," Mathew said. "It is just that a lot of people don't believe an online degree is a real degree,"

Sam laughed. "Don't be silly. Surely an online one might be more *worthy* than a normal degree in a way. You still have to do all the normal work of a degree and balance a full-time job or family commitments and whatever else you do on top of it,"

"You really are amazing," Mathew said.

Sam just looked into Mathew's deep, stunningly beautiful eyes and he leant forward a little. He so badly wanted a kiss but Mathew moved away.

"Sorry. I just know if I start kissing you I don't know if I'll be able to stop,"

Sam's heart skipped a few beats. "Would that be so bad?"

"In public, yes," Mathew said grinning.

Sam went over to the machine and picked up his own bowling ball, he bowled and got a perfect strike.

"And that's it's done," Sam said.

He loved seeing Mathew's face light up as they both grinned, laughed and Sam really knew this was going to be a great night that would hopefully end up with Mathew in his bed.

Hopefully so they could do a lot more than kissing and hugging and everything else that Sam had fantasised about for years and years.

CHAPTER 10
19th April 2023
Strood, England

Mathew couldn't believe how much he had flat out enjoyed, loved and treasured tonight. Of course Sam had won the bowling match and Mathew had really enjoyed just being with someone real that actually cared about him for a change.

Normally up in London his friends, peers and bosses only cared about him for what they could give him and how he could positively impact the agency's bottom line. But whenever he was with sexy, beautiful, wonderful Sam everything was different, in a very, very good way.

After the bowling, Mathew seriously liked how Sam wanted to walk down by the river on the little concrete pathway that was raised high(ish) above the mudflats below. The River Medway was churning, splashing and swirling tens of metres beyond the mud flats.

Mathew hadn't been for years and the last person he had bought was a woman, but it was great holding Sam's soft hand in his. It felt a lot more natural and right and a lot greater than he had expected.

He still so badly wanted to ask Sam to be his model in the campaign but he realised he was starting to fall for Sam too much. It had only been this week Mathew had realised how much, how long, how badly he had seriously liked Sam back at school.

And he had certainly only become more attractive with age.

Mathew gently rubbed Sam's hand and loved the feeling of passion, attraction and sexual tension flow between them. All Mathew wanted to do right now was kiss and make out with Sam, but that wasn't fair on Sam.

Sam deserved a guy better than him. Of that Mathew didn't have any doubt about, yet his job, his world and his future was at stake.

Mathew hugged Sam tight. "You're beautiful,"

Mathew liked how Sam blushed in the weak light of distant streetlamps. He looked so cute, sweet and innocent and that was exactly why Mathew liked him a lot more than he should have.

"What are your plans after uni?" Mathew asked wanting to make small talk for a change.

Sam started to walk on slowly and Mathew followed him and wrapped his fingers around Sam's slightly smaller hand.

"I don't know. The normal I think, do a Masters,

get a job as an assistant psychologist and help people improve their lives," Sam said.

"Amazing,"

"But why don't you tell me what's on your mind," Sam said. "You've been stressed out all night,"

Mathew seriously hated that this was the moment he was going to have to ask Sam what he had been dreading. He had been working all day to try and find out another solution but no modelling agency was available within their budgets on such short notice. That was why he was really stressed.

He was trying to save his job and his relationship with Sam. But he couldn't have both so he chose his job.

"I just need to find some models in the next two days before I lose my job. This damn Fashion Company has my marketing agency by the balls and now my boss has been fired if I pull it off then I get a promotion,"

"Cool," Sam said. "Surely there are some models you can get. Or ways you can get students for models like universities and whatnot?"

"True but HR needs to sort out those contracts because they aren't normal models and I hate my job at times,"

"Could I help?" Sam said. "A lot of people have said that I look like a model,"

The simple innocent question smashed into Mathew like a car crash and he knew there was no way to back out now. He was done for and he really had to choose between his job and Sam.

Sam was so sweet, innocent and Mathew had been falling for him for years at school and they might have reconnected only two days ago but Mathew just felt like he had been falling for Sam for far, far longer than that.

Sam was his soulmate and he had never wanted to take a relationship as seriously as he did with Sam. Mathew really didn't want to lose Sam.

But he didn't want to lose his job either. He had stupidly high rent to pay, he had to pay for his online degree and he needed to money to live on.

He had to choose his job no matter how badly his brain was telling him not to, but like any good business deal Mathew knew he couldn't accept Sam's offer straight away.

"Really? I won't lie you are a wonderful man. I mean it, you are stunning," Mathew said meaning every word of it. "Would you really want to wear a bunch of strange clothes and pose in seductive positions?"

"Would you be in the room?"

"Yes I would be supervising the entire shoot and at this rate I would be behind the camera,"

"See I told you that Media Studies taster session wouldn't be a waste," Sam said.

Mathew nodded. It was amazing that Sam had cared enough about their conversation to actually remember something as simple and innocent as that.

"I'll do it if it helps you," Sam said.

Mathew hugged the beautiful man he was falling for. He really did care about him and he was definitely going to make sure Sam got paid for this emergency work because it was what needed to happen.

And if it all came out that he had only wanted to see Sam again to save his job, Mathew really didn't want Sam to walk away with only a broken heart.

As much as it would kill Mathew himself to lose such an important part of the life he wanted to build for himself.

CHAPTER 11
19th April 2023
Rochester, England

Sam was so damn excited that he was going to be a model for beautiful stunning Mathew tomorrow so as he pulled up outside his house in his little black Ford-something, he just looked at Mathew.

Even in the dim light of the streetlights Mathew still looked so kissable, so amazing and so hot that Sam was really having to fight the urgent to kiss him.

Mathew just couldn't believe how sensational a man could look in a white shirt, black trousers and black shoes. It only highlighted how fit, sexy and brilliant Mathew's fit body was.

A body that Sam so badly wanted to kiss, touch and do so many amazing things to, that he simply hadn't been able to do before to a man.

Mathew grinned at Sam. "Are your parents' home?"

Sam shook his head and realised how much like

teenagers they must have sounded. It was one of the pains about living at home during university break but Sam didn't care.

"No, they're out all night," Sam said.

Mathew placed a large manly hand on Sam's knee. Sam grinned because all his wildest dreams were starting to come true and he was surprised he wasn't shaking anywhere near as much as he thought he would be.

"You're shaking," Mathew said. "We don't have to do this if you don't want to,"

Sam shook his head. "No. I want to do a lot of things with you, it's just I never had the chance to kiss or do anything with a guy before,"

Mathew took the hand away but Sam grabbed it and placed it firmly back on his knee.

"Wait," Mathew said. "Before we get too carried away, let's just talk and you can relax a little,"

Sam really didn't want to wait any more than he had to but he supposed Mathew had done this plenty of times before with men and women and this probably wasn't even his first time with a virgin.

Sam turned off the engine and made sure the street was empty. It was with only the odd stray cat running in-between the parked cars and one even "sunbathed" in the orange light of a nearby streetlight.

"What's kissing like?" Sam asked, seriously embarrassed about the innocence of his question.

Mathew smiled. "You really haven't kissed

anyone before, have you? I thought you and Isla would have kissed at least once when you were going out,"

"That was the plan but I couldn't kiss a girl. I couldn't really bear the thought of it,"

Sam liked how Mathew nodded like it was no big deal and that Sam had nothing to be ashamed of. It was only now that Sam was realising how many missed opportunities he had missed out on as a teenager because he hadn't been Out. He wasn't sad or annoyed, he just supposed that was how things worked out sometimes.

Mathew leant closer, so close that Sam grinned as he smelt all Mathew's manly musk, sweat and rich earthy aftershave that drove Sam insane.

"Kissing can be slow, tender and passionate. Or it can be insanely hot, messy and primal as two people attracted to each other are so into the other person that they can barely keep their clothes on,"

Sam gasped as Mathew slowly and gently slid his hand up his jeans and he couldn't believe this was finally happening. His wayward parts went rock solid and his heart pounded in his chest.

Mathew's hand stopped at the base of his cock and Sam was so badly wanted to be kissed, to be fucked and to have the most magical time ever.

Then someone knocked on the car window.

It was Isla and Toby returning from their own date.

Sam seriously couldn't believe that out of all the

things that could have happened, all the things that could have gone wrong, it was his brother and his best friend that had spoiled this for him.

He was not impressed.

And as he focused on the smiling faces of Isla and Toby, he felt his wayward parts go as soft as butter and the moment was gone. He was even more horny than ever and as Mathew got out the car to talk to the interferers Sam just knew his chance for romance, sex and kissing had passed.

Well and truly passed.

Little did Sam realise that his best friend and brother had just saved him considering what was going to happen tomorrow.

CHAPTER 12
20th April 2023
London, England

Mathew seriously hadn't felt as horny as he was feeling right now for years. All he wanted to do was run off to the toilets and pleasure himself but he was way too busy with Sam and the entire campaign to deal with anything.

Mathew had paid for Sam's petrol and parking and Tube train this morning as Sam had been great enough to drive them up to London. Then they had come into the Marketing Agency and took setup, thankfully Mathew had already set up the green screen before he left last night so everything was set up for this morning.

Mathew had loved seeing Sam's face lit up at all the displays, rooms and different fashion products the marketing agency had at its deposal. He had had the exact same reaction when he first started and it was one of the things he really loved about his job.

They were both in his office and Mathew was more than happy Sam was impressed with his power, station and influence in the agency that he had earned an impressive office with great views of London.

The entire office smelt great with hints of pineapple, watermelon and coconut perfumes and aftershave the marketing agency had wanted Sam to pose with for another campaign.

Mathew had grabbed a massive high-tech camera with more buttons than he knew what to do with earlier from the Camera Department. Why they couldn't do the photograph for the campaign in the first place Mathew didn't know but it was clear the marketing agency wanted him to do this and him only.

"This is beautiful," Sam said.

Mathew looked at the beautiful man he was seriously falling for and couldn't believe how amazing Sam looked in a tailored sleeveless white silk shirt, female black flare trousers and black shoes that actually bought everything together.

It certainly wasn't what Mathew had thought or wanted when he suggested Sam should just try out whatever he wanted for the first few photos so he could get used to modelling. But Mathew couldn't deny Sam looked so hot, sexy and he was glad Sam couldn't see his wayward parts pressing against his own trousers.

"You look amazing," Mathew said getting behind the camera and gesturing Sam to strike a sexy pose in front of the green screen.

Mathew was so pleased Sam was a natural model. He took twenty photos from all different angles and then he had Sam change into the Fashion Company's summer looks.

The first one was a particular favourite of Mathew's that he wished he could keep for himself. It was a cute little number (as his sister might say) of white shorts, white tennis shoes and a tight-fitting but very supportive and comfortable white sportswear top that had the added benefit of showing how fit Sam was underneath.

The marketing department was going to love him and Mathew could almost taste victory.

He also loved seeing Sam topless as he got changed each time.

For the next three hours Mathew laughed, smiled and giggled like a little schoolboy as he watched Sam change into all sorts of amazingly hot, seductive fashion outfits for the campaign.

He had saved the best til last but he was rather surprised that the Chairman of the Board had knocked on the door and wanted to come in.

Mathew rolled his eyes, that made Sam give him a cute little smile, and he gestured the Chairman should come in.

"Um," the Chairman said looking at Sam as he came in and sat on a sofa. "I'm not sure this is the right model for us,"

Mathew bit his lower lip. He had to save this

marketing campaign, his job and his relationship with Sam.

"What do you mean Sir?" Mathew asked. "He looks beautiful, attractive and any woman would want to do him in these photos. And any man would want to look like him so they could get any woman they wanted,"

The Chairman shook his head. "I couldn't disagree more strongly Mathew. You see his chin and cheeks. They are slightly too fat, too asymmetrical and they are not pleasing to the eye,"

Mathew just looked at the Chairman.

"Sir you are being awful towards a temporary employee. That is not right and how dare you say he's ugly. He is beautiful, hot and I liked him,"

"No you don't and you know exactly why I am saying that,"

Mathew really didn't want the Chairman to ruin everything.

Sam came over. "You're just a pigheaded monster that probably only believes women with eating disorders and men with muscle dysmorphia should be models. You're a monster and you are evil,"

"Really?" the Chairman said laughing. "If I of all people are evil then what would you say to your boyfriend or fuck buddy or whatever you people call yourself?"

Mathew really wanted to stop this all but his mouth just wasn't working. It was too dry and this was falling apart too quickly.

"What do you mean?" Sam asked.

"Your boyfriend only got back in touch because he wanted to use you for your looks for this campaign,"

Mathew laughed because the shit had just hit the fan and now everything was falling apart.

His relationship, his job and his future was crashing down around him.

CHAPTER 13
20th April 2023
London, England

Sam flat out couldn't believe what the hell was happening. He felt like the entire room was spinning, the world was collapsing out from under him and everything he thought he knew was a complete and utter lie.

He damn well knew that things were moving too quickly. He just knew that Mathew used people and now everything was going wrong because Sam had been stupid enough to fall in love with such a beautiful, hot, sexy man that he had been in love with for years at school. And ever since.

"You did what?" Sam asked.

He just looked at Mathew with his perfect body, smile and charm but even Sam could tell he was having to force it up. Almost like Mathew was trying to put on a performance. Had their entire relationship been a performance so Mathew could get dumb photos?

"I didn't mean it like that," Mathew said.

Sam shook his head as the old man left the room because he clearly had achieved his aims. Maybe the old man only wanted to make Mathew failed but even if that was true, Sam seriously didn't care. How dare Mathew use him like this?

"Then how the hell did you mean it?" Sam asked gesturing to the green screen and everything else around them.

"I don't know," Mathew said. "At first yeah I only wanted you for the campaign but you're amazing. Over the past few days I've realised how much I have always loved you,"

"Then why didn't you say anything when we were at school together?" Sam asked.

"For the exact same reasons you didn't. We couldn't have been together or gay at school because we were different people in different social groups and yeah. It never would have worked,"

Sam supposed Mathew just might have been right but it was still outrageous that Mathew had only ever wanted to use him.

Mathew came over to him and Sam so badly wanted to run away and cry and just hate Mathew for causing him so much pain and anger.

"All I have ever wanted!" Sam shouted. "Was for a guy to love me, kiss me and show me the love I have always wanted,"

Mathew threw his arms up in the air. "Well tough

shit because this is the real world sammel. Real people don't have love. Real people don't have lasting relationships. Real people have hookups,"

"Bullshit," Sam said walking towards the door.

Mathew gripped his wrist and then instantly left go as he probably realised how he was acting.

Sam just looked at Mathew in horror. "You know Mathew when we were at school together I fell in love with you because you were beautiful like you are now. But I really loved you because you were smart, kind and one of the best people in our entire school,"

"You know I'm that same person," Mathew said.

Sam laughed. He couldn't believe Mathew actually had the balls and delusions to think that. Maybe he was an idiot.

"How many friends have you lost? How many relationships have you doomed? How many family events missed? All because you wanted a meaningless senior job in the end," Sam asked actually wanting to know the answer.

Mathew looked at the ground.

"Exactly," Sam said opening the frosted glass door. "You have given so much to this job and career and you have never found a balance,"

"I make more money than you,"

Sam gave him a mocking clap. "Congrats but you miss the point of life. We all need work and money to survive and we need work that gives us purpose and meaning. And yet we need joy, friends and loved ones to make that survival mean something,"

Mathew shook his head. "I will get that eventually, one day, when I am the most successful I possibly can be,"

Sam actually felt sorry for Mathew because he didn't doubt for a moment the Mathew he loved and had cared about for years was still in there.

"Good for you," Sam said, "just don't call me when it happens because I am done and I hope you find a boyfriend or girlfriend that can tolerate being a mere object to be used. Because you won't see me never,"

Mathew's eyes widened but Sam didn't care (or at least he made sure that Mathew didn't see his pain inside) and Sam just left the office.

He went down the corridor for a moment and waited to see if Mathew cared enough to chase after him. He didn't. Not that Sam really expected that he would.

And then as soon as he went out the marketing agency buildings Sam went into a public restroom and he just let it all out.

He had lost the man he loved and at this rate Sam doubted he would ever be kissed in his life.

CHAPTER 14
20th April 2023
London, England

As soon as beautiful, precious Sam left his office, Mathew just collapsed onto a massive sofa and he wanted to scream, shout and just rip into the green screen. He had never wanted this, he had never wanted to hurt Sam and he had never wanted Sam to find out.

Mathew just forced himself to take deep breathes so he could relax and calm down. He felt like an idiot, a wreck and like he was the most monstrous person in the entire world because he knew he was.

He always felt like this when he lost a friend and he hated losing friends. Mathew didn't doubt none of his friends would believe him but he did love them, he really truly did because they were his friends. The people he could have a laugh with on a sunny day, the people he could cry with on a rainy day and the people he could go out and play with on snowy days.

His friends were his life.

But Mathew didn't deny that his friends were always right about him and his ways and how he treated people. Mathew supposed it was all because he hadn't grown up with a lot of stuff, his parents were always poor and his parents had never really had the work ethic to change their lives.

Mathew seriously didn't want to live in some mould-infested social housing rubbish so he had always been determined to work hard and not play at all. He wanted to be rich, powerful and he wanted to give his children anything they ever wanted.

Of course that all depended on him actually getting a boyfriend or girlfriend in the first place. Something that was proving to be next to impossible because Mathew had to change his ways.

He buried his face in his hands and couldn't work out how to change. He had to focus on being a better person but there was no way out of this nightmare. Mathew supposed the logical thing to do was to quit and not go after the busy Board of Director job and move back down to Medway.

That would surely prove that he was serious about his life and his love and his determination to always respect Sam. But he couldn't do that at all, he had to do something more meaningful and he didn't want to give up his position here because if he did that then surely his life was meaningless.

Someone knocked on the room.

"Come in," Mathew said.

A moment later a very tall woman wearing a red dress and a beehive hairstyle came in grinning.

"Good afternoon darling," the woman said.

As soon as she started talking Mathew recognised her voice as one of the HR people he normally had to order things from on the phone.

"I see that you have had a minor problem with one of the models," the woman said. "Well I am here to tell you all the photos you took today have been ruled illegal because he didn't sign his Model Release form before he started,"

Mathew gasped. This so couldn't be happening to him.

"And when I tried to catch the nice man on the way out he told me to f-off. I suppose that is something that you did,"

Mathew shook his head. He had ruined his relationship with the only man he had ever truly cared about for nothing. All because of bloody paperwork.

"Can we fix this?" Mathew asked.

"Negative," the woman said. "Normally I would find a way to forge the man's signature using him signing the Visitor Logs but the Old Man has ruled that cannot happen. I think he wants you to suffer,"

Mathew stood up. He couldn't believe that the damn Chairman of the Board was actively trying to destroy his life. All Mathew had ever wanted was to work for this marketing agency, give the company his all and now the agency itself was trying to destroy him.

It was pathetic.

But as the woman just looked at him for a reason Mathew didn't know he supposed this was exactly what he deserved because Sam was right. He did only use people and that had to change.

Mathew just had no idea how to change his ways and become a better person.

"And I was ordered to come here because the Old Man wants to talk to you immediately,"

Mathew rolled his eyes because this surely couldn't have gotten any worse but he had a strange feeling that it really was about to get far worse than he ever could have imagined.

CHAPTER 15
20th April 2023
London, England

As Sam drove along the long endless motorway with thick oak trees lining it and everyone else in their black, blue and white cars of different shapes and models driving calmly, he just couldn't believe how the hell that had happened.

He had made sure he was cried out but he still didn't dare talk, even to himself in case his voice wobbled and broke like he had a feeling it would at a moment's notice. He flat out hated how Mathew had used him.

But he did sort of understand it as well.

Sam didn't understand it enough to forgive him but he supposed if he was really honest he could see why Mathew thought he needed to use others. Even when they were back at school it was hardly a secret how poor Mathew was.

Mathew had never known it but something that

Sam flat out loved about secondary school and Sixth Form was everyone liked him, so Sam could easily float between friendship groups. And people said things in his presence that they didn't dare say to others.

Sam had heard a lot of things about beautiful, sexy Mathew. Even Mathew's own best friends mocked him for being so poor and his parents were good enough that Mathew and everyone loved them. But they couldn't exactly give Mathew too much.

So Sam could sort of understand how and why and what Mathew was prepared to do to get ahead in life, and he really could see the appeal and fear that came from never ever wanting to end up like his parents.

This just wasn't the way.

Sam pulled over into another lane, overtook a small white car and then pulled into the lane again so he wasn't lane-hogging.

He clicked the hand-free console on his dashboard and called an old friend that he hadn't heard from for years. Sam just hoped Lewis hadn't changed his number, he wasn't even sure why he had Lewis's number in the first place.

He knew that Lewis' friendship with Mathew had ended over a woman and they had even fought before they agreed to never see or talk or contact each other again. But they had been extremely close once and Sam wanted to know something.

He wanted to know if Mathew had always liked

him. If Mathew had told anyone anything back in the day he would have told Lewis.

He answered. "Hello?"

"Lewis Chapman?" Sam asked. "This is Sam from secondary school,"

"Oh yeah. Hi Sam how are you? How did you even get this number man?"

Sam laughed as he slowed down because a lorry up ahead. "I have no idea, I think you gave it to me once. Anyway, have you spoken to Mathew since school?"

"Yeah man course I have. A great guy but it was a shame when he got that new fancy job up in London he sort of became a bit of a slime ball,"

Sam was surprised.

"And before you ask man, me and Mathew patched things up when he started telling me his interest in boys. I was curious but yeah, I ain't no gay I can tell you that much,"

Sam knew Lewis wasn't being homophobic at all but it was a great image him and Mathew doing something together. He was certainly saving that image for later on when he was alone in his bed.

"Okay," Sam said, "about that what has Mathew told you about him being Bi. I'm just wondering if there's a reason why he would try to sabotage a relationship and want to use people?"

Sam started to speed up a little as he pulled into another lane and overtook that stupid English lorry driver. He had never understood why the foreign lorry drivers always got the blame, in his experience the English were the worse.

"Yeah actually mate. He was drunk as fuck one night and he was really really horny. All he kept banging on about was you and how he wanted to fuck you so hard you couldn't walk properly the next day,"

Sam grinned. He certainly wouldn't have minded if Mathew wanted to do that to him but at least he knew Mathew had always liked him, been attracted to him and maybe Mathew had even loved him. Or loved him as much as schoolboys could.

"Thanks," Sam said about to hang up.

"Mate? Are you finally together? If so then massive congratulations, you were always a cool guy at school and yeah, hope it goes well,"

"Thanks," Sam said hanging up.

Sam felt a little better now that he knew that Mathew had always had a thing for him and it actually made him like Mathew even more.

But then he realised he was all alone again just in his car and there was no one to grieve with, talk to or admire.

Sam was completely alone and now he had no idea at all how he was going to help Mathew and fix their relationship.

The very relationship he had wanted for years and he had walked out on.

CHAPTER 16
20th April 2023
London, England

Mathew seriously hated the sick sinking feeling he had in his stomach as he went into the massive Board Room with its freshly polished conference table, 360-degree view of London and the Chairman was sitting perfectly straight.

Mathew noticed the large range of coffee, teas and more exotic soft drinks that he didn't recognise on the table but he didn't focus on them. He was a lot more concerned about the Chairman and what the hell he wanted with him.

It couldn't have been about his work performance, it couldn't have been about his work behaviour and Mathew had no idea about what else it could have been. He was the perfect worker.

"Thank you for coming to see me after all of that," the Chairman said.

Mathew shook his head, folded his arms and he

made sure to block the Chairman's view of London. He never would have normally been so disrespectful to his boss but after the stunt the Chairman had pulled he wasn't too interested in his feelings.

"What do you want Sir?"

"You to resign," the Chairman said.

Mathew laughed. He couldn't quite believe how stupid he had been from the start with Miranda being a hardass and awful person and he didn't doubt the Board position had just been a way for the Chairman to use him even more.

"Why?" Mathew asked.

"Because," the Chairman said pouring himself another cup of coffee, "you are a good worker. You might actually be able to run this entire agency one day but that would mean you turn into me,"

Mathew shrugged. "And that would be a problem Sir? You're worth a hundred million pounds, you have businesses all over the globe and you have a loving wife and three kids,"

"That's funny," The Chairman said like Mathew had said the funniest thing ever. "My so-called loving wife is always having affairs and hell I even pay for her and her boyfriends to go away together,"

Mathew had no idea about this so he took a seat.

"And my three adult kids. Well my son doesn't talk to me period and the last time we spoke was five years ago when him and his boyfriend were moving to France,"

Mathew was more than glad he had a gay son so

at least he doubted the Chairman was a homophobe.

"My other son is turning into me and he's about to dump the love of his life because he's an idiot. And my daughter, Jesus just I love her. She's in drug rehab and I don't doubt she'll be there for another few years,"

"I'm sorry,"

The Chairman wiped his eyes. "No, don't be. This is my point to you. You can get rich, all-powerful and run a massive international company that makes you more millions than you could ever think possible but there is a price,"

"How would you describe your price?" Mathew asked making himself a cup of coffee.

"I am alone with no real family and even my employees aren't that bothered,"

Mathew smiled because he wasn't lying there.

"So I want to give you a choice," the Chairman said. "Look around this Board Room and if you can truly, truly see yourself hear running the entire company for the next forty, fifty years then stay and doom your life forever,"

Mathew both did and didn't like the sound of that in the slightest. All he really wanted was beautiful, sexy Sam and a life with him.

"Or if you want a life filled with happiness and love and sex that actually means something. Leave today, I will pay you two years' wages and I will give you a glowing reference to whatever job you apply for in the future,"

Mathew nodded but he leant forward. "Why are you doing this for me? You have thousands of employees, probably hundreds of thousands all over the world. Why me?"

"Because," the Chairman said, "I haven't done a lot of good in my life. Just let me save one single person before I retire next year. What do you say?"

Mathew looked around and he grinned as he imagined all the millions and power and sheer authority he could have over this amazing company as he led meetings and teams of brilliant people. He could do so much for this company and he could continue to create such breathtaking designs and campaigns for so many clients.

But he understood that he couldn't have the man he loved. He couldn't see Sam's beautiful smile, he couldn't see Sam's wonderfully fit body that he just wanted to hug and touch all day and most importantly he couldn't give Sam his first anything.

Mathew looked around and realised this actually wasn't what he wanted.

All he actually wanted in life was to be better off than his parents and he already was. He could easily sell his London flat for the price of most small houses back in Medway and it wasn't exactly like Kent had a lack of businesses to work for.

He could still make money, make friends and he could actually be with the man he loved. He could be with Sam, if he saw how much he was changing and willing to continue changing.

Mathew stood up, filled his pockets with expensive tea and coffee and any other high-end things he wasn't going to have access to anymore. And then he simply grinned.

"I resign,"

CHAPTER 17
21ˢᵗ April 2023
Rochester, England

The next day Sam leant against the cold metal wire fencing of the local basketball court in the local park that no one ever went to. The grass looked a little depressed and the large clouds were dark grey and it looked like it was about to rain.

Sam was only really here because he wanted to talk to Toby alone without anyone, even wonderful Isla because his brother had always been great when he had had boyfriends before and he really needed some advice now.

A few moments later Sam smiled as Toby in his black tracksuit came into the court and Sam passed him the basketball.

"Bro," Toby said, "never in my life have you ever asked to play sports with me. Do you even know how to play Basketball?"

Sam pretended to look offended. "Of course I

do. I dropped PE as soon as I could but I know the rules and come on, how hard can it really be to shoot a hoop,"

Toby gestured to the large rusty red hoop a little to their left and laughed. "Believe me Sammy you cannot shoot that hoop. If you get a hoop we can talk about Mathew all day but if you lose you're stuck watching football with me all day at home,"

Sam shrugged as Toby passed him the ball and he threw it and it went straight into the hoop.

"You were saying?" Sam asked grinning.

Toby went over to grab the basketball and he tried to shoot a hoop. He failed.

"You know what they say Toby, some people have talent and some people are just wannabes,"

Toby laughed as he went over to the other side of the court and tried to shoot again with a bit of running start.

Sam sort of knew that Toby wasn't going to stand still long enough for them to talk so he just wanted to ask his questions.

"Isla must have told you what happened?" Sam asked knowing he had been in the room with Isla when he had phoned her last night. Even now he hadn't really talked to her, he had only mostly cried.

"Yeah," Toby said shooting his hoop.

It missed by a long shot.

"But," Toby said, "I don't know what I can say. What do you think the problem is?"

Sam couldn't believe his wonderful brother was

actually trying to avoid the question so he could focus on his little basketball. It was so typical of him but Sam supposed it wouldn't be bad to use his brother as an idea board.

"So I know Mathew loves his job, he doesn't want to be poor and he's too dedicated,"

Toby focused on the hoop. "Okay I get that, but have you tried calling him?"

"I don't want to speak to him," Sam said and was only realising how angry he still was. How dare Mathew use him.

"I think we've found your problem," Toby said shooting another hoop and failing.

Sam nodded. He had sort of always known that was his major problem with Mathew, he simply didn't like being used and that was what stung so badly.

Sam had dealt with idiots before, never in relationships but he had dealt with friends and other people that had bullied him, said horrible things and were just awful people all round.

But he had never been betrayed this bad before, he hated how much it hurt.

Sam looked at his brother trying and focusing and he looked so determined to actually shoot a hoop. Maybe that was what Sam needed to do with his relationship with Mathew.

Maybe he needed to focus less on the fact he was betrayed because it definitely hurt, but it didn't have to define him. And if he really did care and even love Mathew then surely he could look past that fact because Mathew had done it for a reason.

A very, very bad reason but a reason that Sam knew could change so he didn't do it again.

"You actually like him don't you?" Toby asked. "After everything he put you through these past two days, you actually like him,"

Sam grinned as he took the basketball away from Toby again. "I know it isn't logical but when I think about him I feel light, happy and I want to see him again,"

"Then maybe you are a fool but I get it. I love Isla, always have since you two first became friends and it's why I was so supportive when you came out,"

"Oh what because you finally knew you could date Isla without there being a chance me and her would fall in love," Sam said really not wanting this to be true.

"Of course big brother and that was always the plan," Toby said knowing he didn't want it to be true. "And that's why I love Isla because she is kind, great and it means she can be part of our family officially,"

Sam laughed because that so wasn't needed. Isla was family, so Sam threw the ball and he shot a hoop.

"Oh come on," Toby said.

Sam grinned because now he was ready to call Mathew. He wanted to find him, talk to him and just see if there was ever a chance for them to get back together.

He was ready because if this chaos had taught Sam anything it was that sometimes people did bad things for okay reasons. And he really did believe in Mathew enough to know he wouldn't betray him again.

Little did Sam realise just how much had changed and just how much trouble he was going to have trying to talk to him.

CHAPTER 18
23rd April 2023
Rochester, England

Mathew was a complete and utter failure.

He knew that beautiful sexy Sam had been trying to call him for days and even trying to phone him multiple times an hour that sometimes Mathew had simply wanted to see the record for the most calls in a single hour. He was rather impressed the record was twelve, a call every six minutes like clockwork.

But Mathew flat out didn't want Sam to see him, talk to him or even acknowledge he was alive because he was nothing but a complete and utter failure.

Mathew had wanted to quit his job, sell his London apartment that went for a lot more money than he ever thought possible and start to live a good normal life, but that wasn't happening.

He was currently sitting at his old brown oak desk in his old bedroom at his parent's house. The room hadn't changed in two years and it was still damp, musty and stuffy.

The air smelt a little of the dampness but that was just the area and property itself. Then there were just the odours of his minty, watermelon and grapefruit air fresher that he had sprayed to try and make the room better but it wasn't working.

Mathew felt like such a failure. He wanted to find a place to rent or buy and he wanted a job and he had applied for tons in the Kent area. He had applied for jobs as far North as Northfleet to as far south as Dover to as west as… he actually didn't know many West Kent places.

It was all a nightmare and he had only heard from a few job places but they had all rejected him because he was "overqualified". What the hell did that even mean? Mathew had worked with some of the biggest companies in the world, he had created great campaigns for them and he knew marketing inside and out. Why wouldn't he just get a job?

Mathew just knew if Sam found him like this living in his parent's place yet again, he would be a failure. He didn't want Sam to know that the hot, confident guy he had fallen in love with was a nobody.

He saw Sam phone him again and he went to decline the call when he stopped. He actually didn't want to decline the call but he didn't want to answer it either.

Mathew had always known that Sam had liked him a lot at school and he had seriously liked Sam too. At school he was a popular, sporty jock with a so-called perfect body and "beautiful" blond hair according to the girls he had dated.

Mathew could understand his hair and body and intelligence were reasons why Sam had liked him, Sam had said as much, but he wasn't successful at school, he wasn't rich at school and he wasn't any better off than he was now.

Mathew stood up and stretched as he realised that maybe, just maybe he really didn't need to be amazing, over-the-top and rich to be happy. He had seen that wealth had destroyed the Chairman's life so maybe this was what he meant about being happy by finding love.

As Mathew looked down at his phone, he felt his stomach fill with butterflies as he accepted the call and there was only a single question that he wanted the answer to.

"Why do you love me?" Mathew asked.

He loved that he could hear Sam's beautiful breathing on the end of the phone. It was great knowing that Sam was alive, okay and wanted to talk to him. Mathew couldn't believe how damn much he had missed this beautiful man and he never wanted to leave Sam ever again.

"I love you because your body is amazing, your blond hair is to die for but honestly, because as I said before, you are the kindest, most amazing person I have ever met. I don't care if you're rich, I don't care if you're a millionaire and I seriously don't care if you live in London,"

Mathew nodded even though Sam couldn't see him.

"Do you remember Mr Shepley's old saying about love? The one above the room that my friends joked about once," Sam asked.

Mathew grinned. "He always used to say that home was an illusion because all of your homes are where we feel alive, loved and safe,"

"I feel that way when I'm around you and that is all I need," Sam said.

Mathew forced himself not to cry regardless of how damn impossible that was going to be.

"I am sorry," Mathew said. "I was an idiot but I promise I am changing. I sold my apartment back to the building manager, I quit my job and now I'm back in Rochester,"

He didn't blame Sam for being so silent on the other end of the line. This was a hell of a shock for him too.

"And," Mathew said, "I truly, truly know that using people is flat out wrong and I *know* I don't need to do it ever again. So if you could possibly find it in yourself to forgive me then can I be your boyfriend again?"

Mathew just looked at his phone to make sure the call hadn't been disconnected after a long pause between them. Mathew really hoped Sam wasn't going to say no, all Mathew wanted in the entire world was to be with Sam even if he was poor and a failure.

He only needed Sam to be happy and successful in life.

"Yes," Sam said. "God damn yes I want you and you owe me something anyway,"

Mathew laughed and laughed as him and Sam spent the next three hours talking and planning and joking about the relationship and their plans for the future. Mathew promised never to use people again which he was always going to be, he also planned to find a job even if it wasn't in business and he promised or more like vowed to be the best boyfriend on the entire planet to Sam, the man he truly loved more than anything else in the world.

He might have loved his old job, his business degree and living in London but all that love combined was still only a mere candle compared to the raging inferno that was his love for Sam.

Their love might have been years in the making ever since they had first spoken and seen each other at school but Mathew was just glad that their love was finally happening now. And Mathew seriously knew that if their love could survive secondary school, their years apart and the disaster he had created.

Then their love was going to last a lifetime, all because Sam had wanted his first-ever kiss. Something Mathew was determined to give him more than ever before.

CHAPTER 19
25th April 2023
Rochester, England

The next two days had to be the longest in Sam's life because he had to do some Outreach work that he had signed up for because Kent University was desperate for support and Sam had been so annoyed at Mathew at the time that he just signed up for them. The idea that he could have been busy with Mathew instead just seemed flat out impossible.

But he leant on the back of their black family sofa in the living room and Sam just watched out the massive window waiting for Mathew to finally turn up. He had been home for an hour and he really hoped that Mathew, the beautiful stunning man he loved was actually going to turn up.

There weren't many cars parked out on the road, which was strange for a weekday evening. There were only some large black cars that the neighbours had bought recently because they were apparently the latest cool thing to have.

Sam smiled at the poor dog walker that passed him. He even got a few tails wagging from the various Yorkshire Terriers around the road, Sam had to admit he probably looked weird but he didn't care. The moment he saw beautiful Mathew he fully intended to rush to the front door.

Sam laughed as Isla and silly Toby tried to tickle his toes as they were sitting either side of him, and he felt the happiness, bestest and most delighted he had been in years. His brother and best friend were in love and so was he.

And those three hours had flown by a few days ago. He had really enjoyed, loved and treasured talking to Mathew because he was clearly sorry, he wanted to change and he was seriously making an effort to become a better person.

Sam believed he would without a shadow of a doubt.

The rich aroma of peanut butter cookies filled the air as his Mum finished cooking up another batch and Sam just grinned as a car pulled up outside.

Sam rushed to the front door.

He smiled like a little teenage boy as he watched Mathew get out of the car and slowly come up the driveway towards their house. Sam couldn't believe how beautiful, sexy and wonderful Mathew looked. He actually looked how he did back at school. Even now Sam could tell he still played sports or went to the gym and it seriously suited him.

Sam grinned as Mathew stopped in front of him and Mathew wrapped his big, strong, manly hands around his waist.

Mathew moved his lips closer to Sam and Sam immediately felt his wayward parts spring to life like soldiers and he just couldn't believe how sensational the feeling was of being in another man's arms. This had never been a schoolboy crush, a fling or anything else. This had always been real, true love.

Sam moved his lips closer so close that he could feel Mathew's wonderful breath on his lips and then their lips grazed. Sam almost jumped at the sheer chemistry, attraction and electricity that flowed between them.

And then Mathew kissed him.

Sam moaned in pleasure and delight as he tasted Mathew's soft and velvety and silky lips. The kiss was everything that Sam had always wanted it to be and so much more.

The intensity was unreal as was the sheer taste of a real man and all the sexual tension between them went up on steroids.

Sam jumped and wrapped his legs around Mathew's fit sexy waist and Mathew just carried him off upstairs because neither one of them could last any longer. They were in love, they were in passionate love and neither one of them ever wanted this to end.

Not that it actually would because as Mathew carried him upstairs, Sam finally understood what love was really like. After years and years and years of not being out and able to be himself he was finally able to be gay.

And it was far more sensational, thrilling and brilliant than he ever thought possible. And that was an amazing feeling to have as Mathew truly showed him the delights of being gay.

GET YOUR FREE SHORT STORY NOW!
And get signed up to Connor Whiteley's newsletter to hear about new gripping books, offers and exciting projects. (You'll never be sent spam)

https://www.subscribepage.io/gayromancesignup

About the author:

Connor Whiteley is the author of over 60 books in the sci-fi fantasy, nonfiction psychology and books for writer's genre and he is a Human Branding Speaker and Consultant.

He is a passionate warhammer 40,000 reader, psychology student and author.

Who narrates his own audiobooks and he hosts The Psychology World Podcast.

All whilst studying Psychology at the University of Kent, England.

Also, he was a former Explorer Scout where he gave a speech to the Maltese President in August 2018 and he attended Prince Charles' 70th Birthday Party at Buckingham Palace in May 2018.

Plus, he is a self-confessed coffee lover!

Other books by Connor Whiteley:

Bettie English Private Eye Series

A Very Private Woman
The Russian Case
A Very Urgent Matter
A Case Most Personal
Trains, Scots and Private Eyes
The Federation Protects
Cops, Robbers and Private Eyes
Just Ask Bettie English
An Inheritance To Die For
The Death of Graham Adams
Bearing Witness
The Twelve
The Wrong Body
The Assassination Of Bettie English
Wining And Dying
Eight Hours
Uniformed Cabal
A Case Most Christmas

Gay Romance Novellas

Breaking, Nursing, Repairing A Broken Heart
Jacob And Daniel
Fallen For A Lie
Spying And Weddings
Clean Break

Awakening Love
Meeting A Country Man
Loving Prime Minister
Snowed In Love
Never Been Kissed
Love Betrays You

<u>Lord of War Origin Trilogy:</u>
Not Scared Of The Dark
Madness
Burn Them All

<u>The Fireheart Fantasy Series</u>
Heart of Fire
Heart of Lies
Heart of Prophecy
Heart of Bones
Heart of Fate

<u>City of Assassins (Urban Fantasy)</u>
City of Death
City of Martyrs
City of Pleasure
City of Power

Agents of The Emperor
Return of The Ancient Ones
Vigilance
Angels of Fire
Kingmaker
The Eight
The Lost Generation
Hunt
Emperor's Council
Speaker of Treachery
Birth Of The Empire
Terraforma
Spaceguard

The Rising Augusta Fantasy Adventure Series
Rise To Power
Rising Walls
Rising Force
Rising Realm

Lord Of War Trilogy (Agents of The Emperor)
Not Scared Of The Dark
Madness
Burn It All Down

Miscellaneous:
RETURN
FREEDOM
SALVATION
Reflection of Mount Flame
The Masked One
The Great Deer
English Independence

OTHER SHORT STORIES BY CONNOR WHITELEY

Mystery Short Story Collections
Criminally Good Stories Volume 1: 20 Detective Mystery Short Stories
Criminally Good Stories Volume 2: 20 Private Investigator Short Stories
Criminally Good Stories Volume 3: 20 Crime Fiction Short Stories
Criminally Good Stories Volume 4: 20 Science Fiction and Fantasy Mystery Short Stories
Criminally Good Stories Volume 5: 20 Romantic Suspense Short Stories

Mystery Short Stories:
Protecting The Woman She Hated
Finding A Royal Friend

Our Woman In Paris
Corrupt Driving
A Prime Assassination
Jubilee Thief
Jubilee, Terror, Celebrations
Negative Jubilation
Ghostly Jubilation
Killing For Womenkind
A Snowy Death
Miracle Of Death
A Spy In Rome
The 12:30 To St Pancreas
A Country In Trouble
A Smokey Way To Go
A Spicy Way To GO
A Marketing Way To Go
A Missing Way To Go
A Showering Way To Go
Poison In The Candy Cane
Kendra Detective Mystery Collection Volume 1
Kendra Detective Mystery Collection Volume 2
Mystery Short Story Collection Volume 1
Mystery Short Story Collection Volume 2
Criminal Performance
Candy Detectives

Key To Birth In The Past

<u>Science Fiction Short Stories:</u>
Their Brave New World
Gummy Bear Detective
The Candy Detective
What Candies Fear
The Blurred Image
Shattered Legions
The First Rememberer
Life of A Rememberer
System of Wonder
Lifesaver
Remarkable Way She Died
The Interrogation of Annabella Stormic
Blade of The Emperor
Arbiter's Truth
Computation of Battle
Old One's Wrath
Puppets and Masters
Ship of Plague
Interrogation
Edge of Failure

<u>Fantasy Short Stories:</u>
City of Snow
City of Light

City of Vengeance
Dragons, Goats and Kingdom
Smog The Pathetic Dragon
Don't Go In The Shed
The Tomato Saver
The Remarkable Way She Died
Dragon Coins
Dragon Tea
Dragon Rider

All books in 'An Introductory Series':
Clinical Psychology and Transgender Clients
Clinical Psychology
Careers In Psychology
Psychology of Suicide
Dementia Psychology
Clinical Psychology Reflections Volume 4
Forensic Psychology of Terrorism And Hostage-Taking
Forensic Psychology of False Allegations
Year In Psychology
CBT For Anxiety
CBT For Depression
Applied Psychology
BIOLOGICAL PSYCHOLOGY 3RD EDITION
COGNITIVE PSYCHOLOGY THIRD

EDITION
SOCIAL PSYCHOLOGY- 3RD EDITION
ABNORMAL PSYCHOLOGY 3RD EDITION
PSYCHOLOGY OF RELATIONSHIPS- 3RD EDITION
DEVELOPMENTAL PSYCHOLOGY 3RD EDITION
HEALTH PSYCHOLOGY
RESEARCH IN PSYCHOLOGY
A GUIDE TO MENTAL HEALTH AND TREATMENT AROUND THE WORLD- A GLOBAL LOOK AT DEPRESSION
FORENSIC PSYCHOLOGY
THE FORENSIC PSYCHOLOGY OF THEFT, BURGLARY AND OTHER CRIMES AGAINST PROPERTY
CRIMINAL PROFILING: A FORENSIC PSYCHOLOGY GUIDE TO FBI PROFILING AND GEOGRAPHICAL AND STATISTICAL PROFILING.
CLINICAL PSYCHOLOGY
FORMULATION IN PSYCHOTHERAPY
PERSONALITY PSYCHOLOGY AND INDIVIDUAL DIFFERENCES
CLINICAL PSYCHOLOGY REFLECTIONS VOLUME 1

CLINICAL PSYCHOLOGY REFLECTIONS VOLUME 2
Clinical Psychology Reflections Volume 3
CULT PSYCHOLOGY
Police Psychology

A Psychology Student's Guide To University
How Does University Work?
A Student's Guide To University And Learning
University Mental Health and Mindset

www.ingramcontent.com/pod-product-compliance
Lightning Source LLC
LaVergne TN
LVHW011845060526
838200LV00054B/4171